D0231369

For Phil, Sean, Bethany, Joey & Katy.

(mon-mons!) Love you all xxxx

S. W.

For Tom, Kerry & Kenny G!

Book Band: Turquoise
Lexile® measure: 520L

First published in Great Britain 2018
This Reading Ladder edition published 2018
by Egmont UK Limited
The Yellow Building, 1 Nicholas Road, London W11 4AN
Text copyright © Sheryl Webster 2018
Illustrations copyright © Richard Watson 2018
The author and illustrator have asserted their moral rights
ISBN 978 1 4052 8452 3
www.egmont.co.uk
A CIP catalogue record for this title is available from the British Library.
Printed in Singapore
65128/1

Stay safe online. Egmont is not responsible for content hosted by third parties.

Egmont takes its responsibility to the planet and its inhabitants very seriously.
All the papers we use are from well-managed forests run by responsible suppliers.

Series consultant: Nikki Gamble

Monster Rhymes

SHERYL WEBSTER

ILLUSTRATED BY RICHARD WATSON

Reading Ladder

Meet the Monsters

Doris - Page 6

Dragon - Page 10

Troll - Page 18

Doris

Dear Reader, I'm Doris! Please
 DON'T scream or hide.
I may be a monster, but I've *never* lied.

You may think us monsters are big,
 mean and hairy.
With warts on our noses and claws that
 are scary.

Perhaps if I tell you a story or two,

You may change your mind? I'll leave

that up to you . . .

So reader, believe me, we don't *mean* to scare.

Give monsters a chance, and read on . . .

if you dare!

Dragon

Take Dragons for instance, all teeth,
  flames and claws,
Just waiting to gobble you up in their
  jaws.
Is *that* what you're thinking, is *that*
  what they'll do?
This story may show you a new thing
  or two . . .

10

11

There once was a Knight: meet Sir Bob
the Bold.

Bob found a small cave, to escape from
the cold.

Bob saw flames flickering, fiery and
red.

Then a clicking of claws, and his heart
filled with dread.

He glanced at a sign on the wall:
'Amber's Lair.'

'D . . . d . . . dragon!' Bob cried,
spotting Amber . . . right there!

He shook and he gulped. 'Please don't
eat me for lunch . . . '

'I much prefer toast!' Amber said, with
a CRUNCH!

CRUNCH!

CRUNCH!

15

'This jumper should warm you, I hope it will fit.

With my clickety claws, oh I do love to knit!'

Troll

Next up is Troll, who is mean, bad and
smelly,
Feasting on all sorts to fill up his belly.
Humans or goats make a tasty troll
feast.
Is that what you think of when you see
this beast?

Troll's tummy was rumbling, and
looking much thinner,
He whipped out his apron. 'I'll have
goats for dinner.'

The goats spotted Troll's cook book.

What were they to do?

It seemed they were soon to become a

Troll stew!

They trembled with fear as old Troll
licked his lips.
And said to the goats, 'So, how are you
with chips?'

You see Troll LOVES dinner parties.

He thinks they're the best.

And that's why he invited the goats as

his *guests*.

Troll serves the goats' favourite, to fill
up their bellies!
Grass pie, then bug bites in green slimy
jelly!

HOW TO
COOK GOATS
A LOVELY
MEAL

Werewolf

Werewolves are fierce and monstrous
and hairy.

Prowling and making the night-time so
scary.

They bristle their fur. They sneer and
they scowl.

And why, when they see a full moon,
do they howl?

26

One cold starry night a long time ago,
A sharp-eyed young werewolf found
something in the snow.

She gathered some friends and she
taught them to play.

The BIG match was set for the end of
the day.

Werewolf was awesome! She played
like a dream.

She dribbled . . . she scored! 'Go
werewolf team!'

Then the bat striker swooped – it was clearly a foul!
The ball soared from sight, making each werewolf howl.

Now as each full moon comes, you can still hear them cry,
Thinking their ball is that one in the sky.

Vampire

Vampires, like Dracula, have pointy fangs.

They go around biting your necks in their gangs.

All vampires are scary and bloody and gory.

Perhaps you'll find out something more in this story?

Here we see Drac with his mouth
dripping red,
But he hungers for more and he leaps
from his bed.

He sees rows of humans lined up in the queue.

It's a pain in the neck, but he knows what to do.

Drac has to get past them. 'It's time to
   fly!'
So he changes to Bat-Drac and takes
   to the sky.
He flashes his fangs, and on speedy bat
   wings,

Grabs at some bags of his favourite things.

You see Drac LOVES donuts.

'They're so sweet and yummy!'

40

41

Ghost

Ghosts float around you, all spooky
and white,
Giving you chills as they wail through
the night.
Clanking and banging and crying out,
'Woooooo!'
But perhaps there's a reason they do
what they do?

Inside the house there's a strange
clanking sound.

Could it be Ghostie, floating around?

Maybe he's dragging his big heavy chains?

Or . . . could it be soap suds that gurgle down drains?

Gurgle!

Gurgle!

For Ghostie loves washing and getting
things clean.
Sitting for hours by the washing
machine!
He likes all the swooshing, the noise
and the din.
Seeing the clothes tumble round as
they spin.

But drying is Ghostie's most favourite
thing.

He sings with the howl of the wind, as
he swings.

Wooooo!

And now that my story has come to the
end,
can you see that a monster would
make a great friend?